The *Magical* Truths
of Caroline Casey

Joseph P. Rogers

"There are more things in heaven and earth, Horatio, than are dreamt of in your philosophy." -- William Shakespeare

Chapter 1 – Hobnobbing

My name is Caroline Casey, and I can see an entire world that is invisible to everyone else. At least I'm sure that this parallel world is invisible to everyone I know. I would suppose that there are others around who can see what I see and hear what I hear.

Hopefully, someday I will meet another person like me. It would be nice to have someone with whom I could share my experiences.

I certainly can't share my supernatural experiences with my sister, Helen. She is older than I am, so perhaps that's part of the problem. Helen is eighteen years old, and I am fifteen years old. Helen is interested in soccer and dating and going to the mall. None of these things is of interest to me at all.

When I tried to tell Helen about the fairies who live in the woods near our house, Helen laughed at me and told me to grow up. She said that I am immature for my age.

Helen called me a "crazy nutcase." Later that evening, I heard her suggesting to our parents that they make an appointment for me with the psychologist at my high school.

I have often tried to figure out why I can perceive this other magical world. Here are my three main theories:

My first idea was that there is something about my brain chemistry that enables me to perceive other dimensions. If this is the case, it must be a very rare genetic mutation since I have never heard of anyone else having it.

My second theory is theological rather than biological. Perhaps this is a spiritual gift.

My third theory is that, for whatever reasons, I am more open and sensitive to my surroundings. I see things that other persons would be able to see if they would open their hearts and minds.

In any case, I'm glad that I can perceive the magical world. I feel like I'm on an adventure. I never know what is on the other side of the hill.

On the first day of my summer vacation, I had intended to sleep late, perhaps until noon, but my father decided to mow the lawn. Realizing the futility of trying to get back to sleep, I got up, got dressed, and went downstairs for breakfast.

Just as I was finishing my bowl of cereal, my father came inside. He was holding two tennis rackets and a canister of tennis balls. He looked annoyed.

"Caroline, where do these belong?"

"Um, I was going to say on the tennis court, but maybe I'd better not."

"They belong in your room, not on the lawn in the backyard. If I hadn't been paying attention, I could have run over them with the lawn mower."

"I don't know how they got on the lawn!" I objected. "After Helen and I played tennis at the park, I left the rackets and balls on the back seat of the car. You can ask her!"

"I suppose the fairies left the tennis rackets on the lawn," my father said.

"No, rackets would be too heavy for the fairies to lift. The garden gnomes are the most likely suspects."

He laughed. "Caroline, you are a unique character. Just try to be more careful with your things in the future."

"Yes, Father."

After he went into the living room, I rinsed out my bowl, then went out the kitchen door into the backyard. I strode over to my mother's flower garden where, to the eyes of an ordinary person, two gnome statues were decorative ornaments in the garden.

I placed my hands on my hips. "Hob and Nob!"

When there was no reaction, I repeated their names a bit louder.

Nob's head turned slightly toward me. "Hush! We're not supposed to talk or move during the daytime."

"And you're not supposed to leave tennis rackets and balls on the lawn!" I scolded them.

Hob looked at me. "We're sorry, Caroline. Tennis looked like so much fun that we wanted to try. We borrowed your rackets so that we could hit balls against the wall overnight."

"That's fine, but you should have placed the rackets and balls back into the car when you were finished."

"That's what we planned to do," Nob said. "However, we were having so much fun that we lost track of the time. We played almost until dawn. A lady walking her dog almost spotted us. We panicked and dropped the rackets as we ran back here."

"Okay, just try to be more careful in the future," I said, echoing my father.

"We will," Hob promised.

"It has been a few days since I talked to you guys. What's new?"

They both became more animated than was prudent during the daytime.

"The troll!" Nob exclaimed.

"Yes, we need to tell you about the troll!" Hob declared.

"What troll?" I asked the obvious question.

"On Tuesday afternoon, we noticed a very large troll under the bridge at the river."

"We don't think that he saw us or we might not be here to tell the story," Nob added.

"On Wednesday, Thursday, and Friday, we went back to check on him, and he was still there. We don't know how long he has been living there."

"Is he dangerous?"

"A troll is always dangerous, Caroline. He's as big as a bus -- well, a small bus. He has fists like sledgehammers and big teeth that can eat anything."

"Have you ever spoken to a troll?"

"No," Hob said. "I'd like to someday, but I'd have to have a good escape route ready in case things went wrong."

"It's always prudent to have a good escape route ready," Nob agreed.

"I wonder why he's here," I said.

"Who knows? Trolls have their own agenda."

"And he might leave tomorrow or fifty years from now," Hob said. "Trolls are unpredictable."

"As are some gnomes who I know." I spoke with them for a few more minutes, then bid them goodbye. "It's been great hobnobbing with you guys, but I'd better get going. I'll see you later."

That hobnobbing line always amused them. They laughed before resuming their standard poses as garden gnomes. Somehow they were able to sleep in those poses. They would awaken shortly after sunset.

I went back into the house and flopped onto the couch in the family room. I turned on the television and began watching a program about lions on a nature channel. A few minutes later, my sister came into the room. Helen was wearing her soccer uniform and holding car keys.

"Wish me luck," she said as she passed by me.

I jumped up. "Can I go to your game with you?"

"Why? You don't like soccer."

"No, but I like snow cones. I was hoping that we could stop at the snow cone stand on the way to the soccer park."

Helen laughed. "Okay. I'm leaving right now, though."

"That's fine."

I followed her out to our mother's car and hopped into the passenger's seat. It was only a five minute drive to the snow cone stand. I bought a grape snow cone, and Helen got a cherry one.

The soccer park was only a half-mile from the snow cone stand. After parking, we walked across the field together before Helen ran off to join her teammates gathering on the sidelines.

I sat in the bleachers and watched the game for a while, but soon my attention wandered toward the nearby woods. Leaving the bleachers, I walked across the park toward the woods.

I was hoping to spot some fairies. This was the only place that I had ever seen them. My first and most spectacular sighting of fairies had been three years ago.

My parents and I were watching one of Helen's games here at the soccer park. Shortly before halftime, I noticed numerous bright, colorful lights in the nearby woods. I pointed out the lights to my parents, but they were unable to see them.

"There are a lot of fireflies out tonight," my father said dismissively.

"Fireflies only emit white light," I objected. "These lights are red, green, yellow, purple, orange, blue, and white."

"I don't know, Caroline. It's another one of life's little mysteries."

It was a mystery that I intended to solve. When halftime arrived, my parents went to the refreshment stand. I ran across the park and into the woods. Heading directly into the lights, I found myself in a realm of wonder.

Hundreds of fairies were dancing and playing. Most were flying, but many were dancing and running along the ground. Because they were so focused on their own activities, they paid little attention to me. They undoubtedly thought that they were invisible to me or appeared as fireflies.

A few of the fairies, though, realized that I could see them for what they were. They smiled and waved at me, somehow realizing that I was no threat to them.

When I heard my parents calling my name, I waved goodbye to the fairies and ran back to the bleachers, where I received a stern lecture about wandering off by myself in the dark.

I still don't know why so many fairies had gathered in the woods that evening. Since that first encounter, there have been five other times that I have seen fairies in those woods. On three occasions I saw them in the daytime, and twice I saw them in the evening. In each of these sightings, there were only two to eight fairies in the woods.

On each occasion, I tried to speak to the fairies, but I never received a response. Perhaps they didn't speak English. Do fairies have their own language? Or perhaps they simply didn't know what to say to me. They might never have previously met any human who could actually see them.

As I strolled into the woods today, I was hoping to find some fairies. The soccer game was not even at halftime yet, so I had time to explore. I wandered deeper into the woods than I usually went.

It was then that I realized that the woods were eerily quiet. Usually I heard the background music of many birds chirping in the trees, but today no birds seemed to be around. In fact, I realized that I had not seen a single squirrel, rabbit, or any other animal. That was extremely unusual.

A chill ran through the length of my body. I felt very uncomfortable. It seemed like a premonition of danger.

I turned and ran as fast as I could. When I reached the open clearing near the bleachers, I breathed a sigh of relief. Perhaps the danger had only been in my imagination, but perhaps it had been real.

In any case, I returned to my bench in the bleachers where I remained safely seated for the rest of the soccer game, attentively watching like the good sister that I am.

After the game was over, Helen's friend, Amy, joined us in the car. They were going to go to the mall. Amy and Helen invited me to join them, but I declined. Spending several hours wandering through clothing and shoe stores and gawking at boys was not my idea of fun. They dropped me off at home before heading to the mall.

Chapter 2

The Mystery of the Missing Sister

At about six o'clock, my parents and I had dinner -- pot roast and potatoes. Helen was still not home, which annoyed my parents a lot. They liked for us to have dinner together as a family whenever possible.

At seven o'clock, my parents started to become concerned. My mother called Helen's cell phone, but there was no answer. She then called Amy's parents, who had also been unable to reach their daughter.

At eight o'clock, my father picked up his car keys.

"I'm going to the mall to look for her," he said, heading toward the front door.

"I'll go with you!" I hurried after him.

We drove to the mall along the roads that we thought were the most likely way that Helen would take, but we didn't see her car. For over an hour, we walked through the mall. We stopped in some of Helen's favorite stores and showed her photo to the clerks.

A couple of clerks recognized Helen and said that she seemed fine. They did not believe that there was any cause for concern.

When the stores began closing for the night, we left the mall and got back in the car.

"I'm guessing that the car broke down somewhere," my father said. "I'm going to try a different route closer to Amy's house."

We drove about two miles east, then turned onto the river road and headed south. As we passed the stone bridge over the river, I remembered the gnomes' warning about the troll by the bridge.

"There it is!" my father declared excitedly.

My attention shifted from the bridge back to the roadway. About fifty yards ahead, the car that Helen had been driving was parked on the side of the road.

My father pulled up behind the car. We jumped out and ran up to look inside. No one was there. In the backseat, there were several shopping bags with their purchases from the mall.

Father's eyes scanned the area. "I saw some movement in the woods," he said, pointing in that direction.

I looked toward the bridge. "While you check that out, Father, I'd like to check out something over by that bridge."

"We should stay together. I don't want to be searching for both my daughters."

"I'll stay within your sight," I promised.

"All right," he reluctantly agreed.

While he crossed the road and headed toward the woods, I ran toward the bridge. My fear was that while driving home, Helen and Amy had seen the troll and stopped for a closer look. Perhaps the troll had allowed himself to be seen in order to trap them.

When I got close to the bridge, I stopped and peered beneath it. I hoped that I could outrun the troll if he pursued me. However, I did not see anyone under the bridge. It was a clear, bright night with a full moon that provided good illumination.

Cautiously, I moved closer until I was certain that there was no one there. If the troll had captured them, he must have taken them to some secret lair.

"Caroline!" my father shouted.

I realized that I might have moved out of his visual range, and he was upset. As I hurried toward the road, I saw that he was not alone.

"I found them!" he exclaimed joyfully. "They were right at the edge of the woods. That was them that I saw moving between the trees."

"Great!" I breathed a deep sigh of relief.

My father gently guided Helen and Amy toward the road. They both had dazed expressions on their faces. I wondered if they even knew where they were.

"What's wrong with them?"

Helen glanced over at me. "I'm fine."

"You look like a zombie," I kidded her. "I'm afraid that you'll bite me and turn me into a zombie, too."

"Caroline," my father said in a quiet reprimand.

"Well, they do look like zombies." I turned toward Amy. "What happened to the two of you?"

Amy shook her head. "I'm not sure. Helen was driving me home from the mall, and everything seemed okay. As we drove down the river road, though, I started to feel a little dizzy. The next thing I knew we were walking around in the woods."

"I had the same experience," Helen said. "I have no idea how we got from a moving car into the woods."

My father looked at them skeptically. "Was there any alcohol or drug use this evening?"

"No!" Helen declared.

"Absolutely not," Amy said emphatically.

Knowing my ability to discern truth and lies, my father glanced at me, raising a questioning brow. I smiled and nodded to indicate that they were telling the truth.

"Do either of you want to go to the hospital?" he asked them. "Perhaps a doctor should examine you."

"No, Mr. Casey, I just want to go home to bed," Amy said. "I just need to get some sleep."

"That's how I feel, too," Helen said. "I'm so tired that I'll probably fall asleep before we get home."

Upon reaching our car, he opened the back door for Helen and Amy. "You two can rest in the back seat."

He took his cell phone off his belt and called my mother, assuring her that the girls were all right and that we would be home soon.

As I sat down next to my father in the front seat, I asked, "What about the other car?"

"We'll pick it up in the morning. Either your mother can drive me back here, or I'll just ride my bike here."

"I wish that I could drive," I said as we headed down the river road.

"That will be just one more thing for me to worry about."

"I'll be a good driver!" I objected.

"I'm sure that you will be, Caroline. I'm sorry. It's been a long day."

"It sure has."

He glanced back at Amy and Helen, who were sound asleep. "Are you sure that they were telling the truth about what happened?"

"Yes, definitely."

"If they weren't using drugs or alcohol, I don't understand what happened this evening. I wonder if there could have been a carbon monoxide leak in the car?"

"That's possible, I suppose. I don't know much about cars."

My father turned onto Amy's street. After parking, he gently awakened her and helped her walk to the front door. He spoke briefly to her relieved parents before returning to the car.

We drove home and pulled into the driveway. My father and I assisted Helen in getting into the house.

"Hi, Mom," Helen said groggily.

"Where have you been, young lady?"

"Walking in the woods near the river," Helen replied.

"Why?"

"I wish that I knew."

"What does that mean?" my mother asked.

"I don't know," Helen said. "I want to go to bed."

My mother looked inquisitively at my father, who shrugged in response.

"All right, Helen," my mother said. "Go to bed, but we're going to have a long talk tomorrow."

"Fine." Helen started going up the stairs.

I followed her upstairs in case she stumbled, but she was able to reach her bedroom. After tucking her into bed, I went into my own room.

My plan was to lie in bed until my parents went to sleep. Then I was going to sneak outside and tell the gnomes about what happened. This strange incident occurred so close to the bridge that there was likely some connection to the troll. I was hopeful that Nob and Hob could explain what had happened to Helen and Amy.

Chapter 3

The Troll Under the Bridge

That was my plan, but it went awry because I fell asleep and did not awaken until nine o'clock in the morning. The gnomes had returned to their positions as small statues in the garden.

When I came downstairs, I went into the kitchen. Helen's shopping bags from the mall were on the kitchen table. Earlier that morning, my parents had retrieved the car and its contents from the river road.

"Is Helen still asleep?" I asked my father, who was drinking a cup of coffee.

"No," he replied. "We got her up about a half hour ago. Your mother was anxious to get her checked out at the doctor's office. They left a few minutes ago. When they get home, I'm going to take the car to a mechanic to check for a carbon monoxide leak," my father said.

"That's a good idea."

While eating a doughnut and a glass of milk, I formulated a new plan that did not involve the gnomes. I wanted neither to wake them up nor to wait nine hours for them to awaken.

When my mother and Helen returned, I was sitting in the family room reading a mystery novel. I placed the book on the lamp table and went into the kitchen where my mother was starting to tell my father about the visit to the doctor's office.

"Dr. Huggins confirmed that there were no drugs or alcohol in her system," my mother reported. "And he was also able to test her for carbon monoxide poisoning. The test results were negative, so I suppose that there's no need for you to take that car to the auto mechanic."

"I might take it there anyway just to be sure."

"Dr. Huggins had some strange news," my mother said. "He told us that last night three teenagers -- two guys and a girl -- were arrested in the art museum. They broke the lock off the front door and were ransacking the place when the police arrived. The teenagers set off a silent alarm when they broke in."

"And they told the police that they didn't know why they broke into the museum," Helen added. "They were groggy like me and Amy."

"The police took them to Dr. Huggins, and he conducted the drug and alcohol tests," my mother said excitedly. "Their tests were also negative -- just like Helen and Amy!"

"That's weird," my father said.

"I'm still really tired," Helen said. "I'm going back to bed."

I followed Helen to the stairs. As she started to go up the stairs, she glanced back at me.

"You don't need to follow me upstairs like you did last night," she said. "I'm not as tired now as I was then. I'm not going to fall down the steps."

"Perhaps I just enjoy your delightful company." I smiled at her.

She grinned. "Yeah, right."

After seeing that Helen was safely in her bed, I came back downstairs and told my parents that I wanted to ride my bike on the hiking and biking trail that ran near our house. The trail was a popular and safe place for bike riding, so my parents readily consented for me to go.

I got my bike out of the garage and was soon riding along the trail. In a few minutes, I reached the section of the trail that ran parallel to the river. I headed north toward the stone bridge. I needed to investigate what was going on at that bridge.

When I was within twenty yards of the bridge, I got off my bike and leaned the bike against a lamppost. There were seven persons within visual range: two fishermen, a rollerblader, two bicyclists, and a couple having a picnic on a park bench.

If I felt like I was in danger, I would run toward the closest persons. Cautiously, I walked forward toward the bridge, peering beneath it for the troll.

If I had not been to that same bridge on the previous evening, his magical camouflage might have fooled me. The troll was that skillful. However, because I had been there previously, I knew that there was no boulder on the riverbank beneath the bridge.

Now, though, there appeared to be a boulder there. Imagine the odds.

As I took several more steps toward the bridge, I made a quick decision about my escape route. If the troll tried to catch me, I would run toward the couple having the picnic. I was hoping that the troll would not pursue me into such a high-visibility situation.

The troll held his knees tucked against his chest as part of his boulder disguise. I saw his eyes flick toward me as I approached.

I stopped. "Mr. Troll, I can see you there. I have the ability to see magical creatures. I intend you no harm and will not reveal this secret location to anyone. May I speak with you?"

The troll's body unfolded, and he stood up. He was about eight feet tall, and his massive body was heavily muscled. He looked down at me appraisingly.

After a few seconds, he spoke in a deep voice. "Hello. My name is Sylvester."

Upon hearing his name, I started to grin, but I stopped myself. He seemed very calm, and I did not want to risk making him angry.

"Hello, Sylvester. My name is Caroline Casey."

"Hello, Caroline."

"Sylvester is a nice name. However, I'm surprised that you told me your name so soon after meeting me. I know that some persons are concerned about revealing their names because they fear that their names could be used in a magical spell against them."

"I don't fear magical spells," he said. "And I don't think that you are a little witch, though I could be mistaken; no human has ever previously seen me unless I revealed myself."

"Well, as I mentioned, I do have that ability to see magical creatures. I also knew where to look for you. Two gnomes who live in my yard -- Hob and Nob -- told me that you were beneath this bridge."

"Hob and Nob," he repeated their names. "I have heard of them -- two fine fellows from what I've been told."

"Yes, they're great guys."

Sylvester noticed that I was maintaining a cautious distance. Whenever he moved a step closer, I moved a step back.

"You can come closer to me, girl. I'm not going to eat you for lunch."

"Oh, that's good," I replied.

Sylvester frowned. "You actually thought that I might make a meal of you. You certainly don't have a very good opinion of trolls."

"Well, as you might know, in many stories the behavior of trolls is less than admirable."

"In many stories the behavior of humans is less than admirable," he countered.

"That's true," I acknowledged.

I took several steps forward and sat down next to Sylvester on the stone ledge. He looked surprised.

"How do you know that I wasn't lying to you?" he asked. "If I was the awful creature that you feared, I would not hesitate to lie in order to catch you."

Looking up at him, I smiled. "One of my special abilities is that I can always tell when a person is lying. I often freak out my family with this ability. I suppose that it is the gift of discernment."

Sylvester nodded. "That is a good gift to have."

"I have discerned that you are a good man from whom I have nothing to fear."

"For one so young, you seem very wise."

"Thank you."

I felt comfortable sitting next to Sylvester on the ledge. My eyes scanned the area under the bridge.

"Where do you sleep down here?" I asked.

His eyes widened. "I don't sleep under the bridge! I spend most of the day here, but I don't consider it to be my home. I have a room beneath the basement of the town's public library. There's a secret entrance in back of the library."

"That's nice."

"Yes, it works out quite well for me. At night, after the library is closed, I often go upstairs and borrow a book or two. Those books are what I read while I'm here at this bridge."

"Why are you here at the bridge?"

"Sagehorn asked me to stand guard here. He received a report that dark forces had a plot against this town."

"Who is Sagehorn?"

Sylvster laughed heartily. "Surely you are joking, girl?"

I frowned. "I most certainly am not joking. How am I supposed to know who Sagehorn is?"

"I'm sorry," he apologized. "That was impolite of me. In my world -- the magical, mystical world -- everyone knows that Sagehorn is the leader of the elves."

"So he's their king?"

"Essentially -- yes, but Sagehorn doesn't like to be called 'king' because he considers the word prideful. He prefers to just be addressed by his name, but he reluctantly allows persons to call him 'Prince Sagehorn.' "

"Modesty is a good quality."

"Yes," Sylvester nodded.

"Why does Sagehorn believe that dark forces are going to do something here?"

"He has received secret information from someone who lives in a sorcerer's lair. Apparently, this person has decided to change sides -- the person has moved away from the dark side and come to the Light."

"Wow -- that's cool. You have a spy in the enemy's camp."

"I suppose that's one way to look at it." Sylvester smiled at me. "I wish that we had more details, though. All I know is that this sorcerer is going to do something in this town."

"Something strange happened last night!" I said excitedly. "When my sister, Helen, and her friend, Amy, didn't come home from the mall, my father and I went looking for them." I pointed over toward the woods across the road. "My father and I found them wandering around right over there. They were both kind of loopy and didn't know how they ended up in the woods. Helen is somewhat better today, but she's still groggy. I don't know how Amy is feeling today."

"Hmmm." Sylvester reflected upon this information.

"And something unusual happened in town," I added hastily. "Last night three teenagers broke into the town's art museum. They set off a silent alarm, and the police arrested them. Apparently they were groggy like Helen and Amy, and they can't even remember why they broke into the museum."

Sylvester became excited and stood up. "Your sister, her friend, and those teenagers were all affected by the sorcerer's dark magic! He cast a spell upon them in order to get them to do his bidding!"

"Oh!" I was so shocked that I didn't know what to say.

Sylvester was visibly distressed. He began to pace back and forth.

"I don't understand how the sorcerer could have got past me! The wardstones didn't signal any alarm, and all of those stones are intact."

"Wardstones?" I inquired.

"Wardstones are a type of elfstones," he explained. "The elves infuse stones with mystical energy so that the stones do what the elves design them to do. I have placed about two dozen of the wardstones along the borders of this town. Some are along the shores of this river. If a power-wielding person passes near one of the wardstones, they emit a signal that I can hear as clear as a ringing bell."

"But you didn't hear anything?"

"No. My guess is that the sorcerer approached this town cautiously, somehow suspecting that we were watching for him. He could have used a small amount of magic to detect the wardstones without setting them off. There was no way that he could get past them, though." Sylvester glanced across the river. "He probably got as close as he could. Perhaps he stood on the riverbank over there. Then he cast his spell over a long distance. He might have directed his spell at persons on the river road like your sister and her friend. Or he might have simply sent the spell out toward the town, trying to take control of whomever he could. Precisely how this black magic works I could not say."

"Will Helen and Amy be all right?" I asked.

"If this incident was a one-time occurrence, the effects of the spell should soon diminish. However, those young women need to be protected from repeated or prolonged exposure to his black magic."

"I'm going to do my best to protect them," I promised.

"I am sure that you will. You certainly will do better than I have so far. I'm annoyed at myself. If you had not come here today, I would not even know that the sorcerer was now in this area. And I should have been aware of what happened at the museum last night. The library where I stay at night is only three blocks from the museum. I heard some police sirens, but I didn't go to investigate. Sagehorn has indeed appointed a poor guardian in this town." Sylvester lowered his eyes to the ground.

"You're being too hard on yourself," I said, trying to cheer him up. "You have prevented the sorcerer from coming into the town. He has been forced to cast his spells from way over on the other side of the river."

Sylvester sat back down, somewhat mollified. "Nevertheless, I need to stop his black magic completely."

"I'm sure that you will," I assured him.

"It seems that the museum contains some object that is of interest to the sorcerer. He tried to get those three teenagers to steal the object for him, but they were stopped by the police. We will need to determine what he wants in the museum."

"But what about Helen and Amy?" I inquired anxiously. "The sorcerer didn't send them to the museum. Why did he cast a spell on them?"

He shrugged. "Perhaps he tried to send them to the museum, but his spell failed because they were too far away. Or perhaps he sent them on some other mission. When the effects of the spell diminish, your sister and her friend might remember enough to be able to tell us. Although it is also possible that they won't remember anything that happened while they were under his spell. We'll just have to wait and see."

"I want to help," I said.

"You can help by taking good care of your sister. If she remembers anything, you can report that information to me."

"I will, but I'd also like to help even more. I could go to the museum this afternoon. Maybe I can figure out what the sorcerer wants to steal from the museum."

"Caroline Casey, there are thousands of items in that museum. The item that he seeks could be almost anything -- a knife, a sword, a cup, a bowl, a book, a jewel, a painting, a statue -- almost anything."

"Well, it won't hurt for me to take a walk through the museum. Something might catch my eye."

"This could be dangerous, my brave young friend," Sylvester said. "I do not want to place you in danger. The elves and I will take care of this situation."

"Okay," I said, not wanting to argue with him. "I guess that I'd better be heading home. I will keep you posted about what my sister says."

"You are going to the art museum first, though, aren't you?" he said as I walked toward my bike.

I stopped and turned around. "Umm, maybe. I might take a quick tour of the museum before I go home."

He sighed. "I can tell that I'm not going to be able to keep you away from that museum." Sylvester reached into his pocket and pulled out a small, sparkling stone. "Since you are such a determined young lady, I'm going to give you this elfstone."

I walked back to him, and he placed the stone into my outstretched hand.

"It's beautiful!" I exclaimed.

In my hand, the elfstone glowed with a faint blue light. Sylvester looked surprised.

"You have a bit of mystical power, Caroline Casey," he remarked. "The function of this stone is to detect magical, mystical powers. That is why I am giving it to you. If you go to the museum, you can hold it close to different objects and see if the stone reacts. If an object is contaminated by black magic, the stone will usually turn red or orange. If the object has some connection to the elves, the stone will usually turn green. Objects imbued with ordinary magical or mystical energy cause the elfstone to turn blue."

"So I'm just ordinary," I said with feigned indignation.

"You are not an object, Caroline Casey, nor are you ordinary. Very few humans can cause the elfstone to glow at all."

"That's good." I grinned at him.

"Be very careful and don't take any action," he cautioned me. "Just report back to me what you discover."

"Thank you, Sylvester. You can count on me." I placed the elfstone into a secure pocket in my jeans. "I'm sure that Hob and Nob would like to speak with you. They wake up shortly after sunset. They could visit with you here before you return to the library."

"That would be fine. I'd like to meet them. Goodbye for now, Caroline Casey." Sylvester waved as I went back to my bike.

"See you later," I said, waving as I rode away.

I went along the river road, then turned onto the road that led into town. When I arrived at the art museum and locked my bike to the bike rack, it occurred to me that it was going to take a long time to search this large museum. The object that the sorcerer sought could be anywhere inside.

I walked up the front steps leading to the central lobby. The central lobby contained a café and gift shop along with entrances to the main galleries that included American art, ancient art, modern art, European art, African art, Asian art, and a special exhibitions gallery in which the featured exhibit changed every few months. At the present time, Aztec art was the featured exhibit.

Holding my elfstone discretely in my right hand, I walked past paintings, sculptures, photographs, drawings, jewelry, and ceramic art objects. To my surprise, many objects caused the elfstone to glow.

These objects included a sword, suit of armor, a spear, a mask, a small statue, an obsidian knife, a moonstone, a jade figurine, and several other things.

As I was walking through the Aztec exhibit, a guard announced that the museum would be closing in ten minutes. I quickly completed my search of that exhibit. I made a mental note of which galleries I still needed to search.

As I left the museum and rode my bike home, I thought about everything that I had seen and tried to figure out what item the sorcerer wanted.

Chapter 4 – Spellbound

When the gnomes awakened in the early evening, I was seated on the stone bench next to the garden. Their eyes first focused upon me, then scanned the yard for other humans. Seeing that I was alone, the gnomes reanimated themselves and scampered over to me.

"Hi, Caroline!" they chimed.

"Hi, guys."

"Did you have a nice day, Caroline?" Hob asked.

"It was very nice, Hob. I made a new friend."

"Who is your new friend?" Nob inquired.

"The troll under the bridge over the river," I replied with an innocent expression, relishing the anticipated reaction.

"The troll under the bridge!" Hob shouted, then lowered his voice, not wanting to attract attention. "Tell me that you're kidding."

"It's the truth. His name is Sylvester, and he's very pleasant."

"Trolls aren't pleasant!" Nob objected. "And they have names like Spike and Slug, not Sylvester!"

"Well, whether you like it or not, that's his name," I said matter-of-factly.

"What did he say?" Hob asked.

"Why is he here?" Nob inquired.

"Sylvester was sent here by Sagehorn in order to protect this town from an evil sorcerer."

"Oh, if Sagehorn sent him, I suppose that he must be a good fellow," Hob said.

I placed my hands on my hips. "So the two of you know who Sagehorn is. Apparently everyone except me knows that he is the leader of the elves."

"Not everyone," Nob said. "I'm sure that there are a few other persons around who haven't heard of Sagehorn."

"I'm glad that I'm not the only ignoramus."

"Perhaps we should have mentioned to you about the elves and Sagehorn," Hob said sheepishly.

"Yes, perhaps you should have."

"Anyway, you know now," Nob said.

"Right."

"Um, not changing the subject," Hob said, changing the subject, "but I was wondering what the sorcerer is planning to do."

"Sylvester and I think that he is planning to steal something from the museum." I reached into my pocket and pulled out the stone. "Sylvester gave me this stone so that I could find what things in the museum had magical qualities." Holding it in my open palm, I knelt down so that the gnomes could better see the stone.

"An elfstone!" Nob exclaimed with wide eyes.

"A very nice one!" Hob added, clearly impressed.

While in my palm, the elf stone glowed with a faint blue light. "Would you guys like to hold it?"

"Yes, please!" Nob said.

I handed him the elfstone. Nob's eyes sparkled with joy as he examined it. He rotated the stone as he studied it from every angle.

"My turn!" Hob said impatiently.

Nob gave him the elfstone. While Hob was inspecting it, I noticed that the elfstone was slightly different in the hands of the gnomes.

"The stone glows brighter when you guys hold it," I observed. "Apparently you have more mystical power than I do."

"Perhaps just a bit more," Nob said modestly.

"We need magic to maintain our disguise as small garden statues," Hob added. He handed the elfstone back to me. "Thank you, Caroline."

"We very much appreciate it," Nob said.

"Sylvester wants to meet you," I told them. "He will be at the bridge for about two more hours. Then he goes to the public library. He sleeps in a room beneath the basement."

"Sagehorn's representative wants to meet us," Hob said, clearly pleased by this news. "We'd be happy to meet him."

"Yes, indeed," Nob agreed.

Sylvester's connection to the elf prince had obviously raised the gnomes' opinion of the troll.

"I'll go with you and introduce your guys to him, but first I want to check on Helen. I'll meet you here in about fifteen minutes."

I went inside and spoke briefly to my parents, who were seated at the kitchen table eating vegetable soup. They told me that Helen's condition had not changed. If she was not feeling better by tomorrow afternoon, they were planning to take her to the hospital for more tests and scans.

After going upstairs, I went into Helen's room. There was a bowl of soup on a tray on the table next to her bed, but Helen was not paying any attention to it.

"Hey, vegetable soup is one of Mom's specialties," I said. "You haven't touched that bowl."

"I'm not hungry," she said groggily.

"You need to eat in order to get your strength back," I encouraged her.

"I just want to go back to sleep, Caroline. A little while ago, I had a dream in which there was a tall man in a black robe standing on the riverbank. He had black eyes that burned like coals, and he beckoned me to come to him."

A shiver ran through the length of my body. "It was just a nightmare. Don't worry about it."

She stared at me. "I'm not worried about it. I liked it. I hope that he appears in my dreams again when I go to sleep."

This is not good at all, I realized.

"Listen, Helen, I wasn't going to tell you this, but you need to understand what is going on. You have to try to break out of this trance that you are in. You are trapped in a spell cast upon you by an evil man -- by a sorcerer." I proceeded to tell her everything -- about Sylvester, about the elves, about Hob and Nob, and about the teenagers who were arrested at the museum. I showed her the elfstone and explained how I had used it to try to find the magical object sought by the sorcerer.

Helen smiled at me. "That is such a cute little fairy tale," she said moments before falling asleep again.

I sighed with exasperation and walked out of her room. I went downstairs and back out into the yard where Nob and Hob were impatiently waiting.

"Okay, guys. Let's go." I bent down to pick them up.

"Yes!" Hob said enthusiastically. "Let's go see the troll!"

"We're ready to go!" Nob chimed in.

Nob hopped into my left hand, and Hob jumped into my right hand. As I stood up, I staggered a bit because the gnomes were heavier than I expected. My best estimate would be that each gnome weighed about ten pounds.

I placed them onto my bike's handlebars. Hob and Nob sat down on the handlebars. I noticed that their hands seemed to lock securely onto the bike, perhaps using a bit of the magic that enabled them to maintain statue poses for many hours every day.

As I rode down the street, I was glad that it was completely dark. My neighbors would think that I was crazy if they saw me riding my bike with two garden gnomes on the handlebars. Some neighbors probably already thought that I was a little crazy, so I preferred to pass by unobserved.

Soon we were out of my neighborhood and traveling north on the river road trail.

"Are you guys enjoying the bike ride?"

"Yes! It's fun!" Nob declared.

"We've never been on a bike before now," Hob added. "I like the feel of the wind on my face."

"I'm glad that you guys are having a good time."

Since it was after dark, there were few persons still on the trail. We saw only two persons: a man jogging and a woman walking her dog.

Despite being in a dark, isolated location with an evil sorcerer lurking somewhere nearby, I felt safe because of the presence of my two friends. The gnomes were small, but they seemed sturdy, and I was confident that they would defend me with all their might.

When the bridge came within sight, I saw Sylvester emerge from beneath it. He strode forward toward us.

"Good evening, Caroline Casey," he greeted us. "And these two gnomes must be the friends about whom you told me. Welcome!"

Nob and Hob jumped off the handlebars and landed in the grass. They looked up at the troll.

"Pleased to meet you. I am Nob."

"And I am Hob. I'm glad to make your acquaintance."

The troll bowed. "Likewise, gentlemen. Caroline Casey has spoken well of you. I have some gnome friends in the Lake District in England."

"Is that where you are from?" Hob asked.

"Yes. I have moved about quite a bit. I go where I am needed -- where duty calls. I lived for many years in the Swiss Alps. However, I consider home to be the hill country in the Lake District. It's a beautiful area."

"Someday we'll have to visit those gnomes in the Lake District," Nob said.

"Beatrix Potter, the author, lived in the Lake District," Caroline said. "She wrote **The Tale of Peter Rabbit** and some other good books."

Sylvester nodded sagely. "I can well understand how that area would a good setting for imaginative stories."

I pulled the elfstone out of my pocket and offered it to Sylvester. "Here is your elfstone. I used it at the museum, but so many items caused it to glow that I'm not sure which item the sorcerer wants. And I didn't have time to search the entire museum."

Sylvester reached out and gently closed my fingers around the elfstone. "You keep that stone. It is yours. I have many other elfstones. This one might be of use to you."

"Thank you so much," I said. "This is a wonderful gift."

"I'm sure that you will use it well."

I gave Sylvester my report about which items in the museum had caused the elfstone to glow. I also told him which galleries I had not yet searched.

"You have done well," Sylvester said. "I'm going to return to town now and try to get into the museum. If I am able to get inside, I'll more closely examine the items that you mentioned. Perhaps I'll be able to determine which item is of such great interest to the sorcerer."

"He might want more than one item from the museum," Nob suggested.

"That's true," Sylvester acknowledged.

"Can we come with you?" I asked anxiously.

"We want to come, too!" Hob said excitedly.

"Yes, we can help!" Nob declared.

"Nob, Hob, and I could search the half of the museum that I didn't have time to search when the museum was open," I said.

"Hmmm." Sylvester considered this suggestion. "That would save a lot of time. While I'm examining the items that you found earlier today, you could continue the search for additional items." He made a decision. "All right! Let's go!"

The gnomes cheered and clapped their hands, excited about the adventure.

"In order to get into town, we are going to need to take the drainage canal that connects to the river," Sylvester said. "When I remain in one place such as beneath this bridge, I am able to use magic to camouflage myself. However, because I am so large, when I travel from place to place, I need to take inconspicuous routes so that I am not noticed. I don't have enough magic to make myself invisible."

"Does the sorcerer have enough magic to make himself invisible?" I asked.

"He probably does." Noticing the gnomes looking around nervously, Sylvester added, "I'm sure that the sorcerer is not yet on this side of the river. The wardstones will give me a signal when he crosses the border that I have formed with those stones. Sooner or later, he will be coming, though, so we need to be ready to react at a moment's notice."

"You can count on us," I said.

Sylvester smiled. "I know that I can. Well, let's get going."

Chapter 5 – Night in the Museum

With Sylvester leading the way, the gnomes and I followed him as he walked upstream toward the junction of the river and the drainage canal. I left my bike behind back at the bridge because I was familiar with the canal and knew that it would be difficult to ride a bike through it -- too many rocks and other debris. After a heavy rainstorm, the canal would fill with water, but most of the time it was empty.

Upon reaching the canal, we descended down the gradual slope of its stone wall. Sylvester observed that the gnomes were having a difficult time keeping up.

"Would you gentlemen like to ride on my shoulders?" he asked.

"Yes, please!" Nob said, puffing from exertion.

"Gladly!" Hob said.

Sylvester reached down and scooped them up. He placed Hob on his left shoulder, and Nob on his right shoulder.

As we headed toward town, I was amused by how comfortable the gnomes looked perched upon the troll's shoulders. Today the gnomes had gone on both their first bike ride and their first piggyback ride on a troll. I was glad that they were having so much fun.

"This canal has been very useful to me in going back and forth between here and the town," Sylvester explained. "It runs directly behind the library."

In a short while, we reached the library, but continued past it toward our destination. When we were close to the museum, we ascended the canal's sloping stone wall and walked out onto the museum's parking lot, which was empty since the museum had closed three hours earlier.

"Now we need to figure out how to get into this place," I said.

We tried the door marked "Employees only." As we expected, the door was locked. Next we checked the large garage-like door of the loading dock. Exhibits were brought in and out of the museum through this loading dock.

"It's locked," Sylvester said after pulling up on the door. "I could easily break the lock, but I would prefer to find a more inconspicuous way into the building."

"There also might be an alarm on the loading dock door," I said. "It's more likely that the museum's front doors and the employee entrances are connected to the alarm system, but it's certainly possible that the loading dock is also connected."

"Let's go to the main entrance of the building," Sylvester said.

As we reached the front of the museum, it became apparent that we would have to proceed more cautiously. There were still a few persons on Main Street. Of most concern, though, was the police cruiser parked in front of the museum.

A bored-looking police officer leaned against the hood of his car as he talked on his cell phone.

"Oh, no! A policeman!" Nob said.

"What are we going to do?" Hob asked.

"I know that police officer," I said. "His name is Tom Coogan. He's the coach of Heather's soccer team."

"This is a bit of a problem," Sylvester said. "I wonder how long he's going to be here."

"I'll find out."

As I walked out onto Main Street, I noticed that the snow cone stand was still open. Since purchasing a snow cone would give me a good reason for being on the street, I decided to make a quick stop at the stand.

"Hi," I said to the young woman working there.

"Hello," she replied. "You're my last customer of the evening. I was just about to close the window."

"I'm glad that I made it in time."

"What would you like?"

I scanned the numerous flavors on the sign. "Cherry looks good."

After paying her and receiving my cherry snow cone, I said goodbye and then casually sauntered down the street. Tom Coogan had finished his phone call. As I walked past him, I glanced to the side and pretended to be surprised to see him.

"Oh hi, Tom."

"Hi, Caroline. You look like you're really enjoying that snow cone."

"Yeah, it's good."

He grinned. "I had a grape one a little while ago. I wish that the stand was open all night. I'd probably buy a couple of more snow cones."

"Are you out here all night?"

"Yeah, unfortunately. Some teenagers broke into the museum last night. We think that it was some sort of senior prank. That kind of thing happens at this time of year. My captain assigned me to guard the museum tonight in order to prevent any other high school students from trying any more crazy pranks."

"Those crazy kids and their crazy pranks. I'm only fifteen, and I have more sense than those high school seniors."

"You're a good kid. Hey, I heard that Helen is sick."

"Yeah. She has the flu or something."

"Helen seemed fine at the game yesterday."

I nodded. "Yes. Her illness happened all of a sudden -- it seemed to come out of nowhere."

"Well, I hope that she feels better soon," Tom said.

"Thanks, Tom. I'll tell Helen that you asked about her. My father is supposed to pick me up in front of the library in about five minutes, so I'd better go over there. I called him a few minutes ago, so he's probably on his way."

"Okay, bye Caroline."

"Good night." I waved as I headed down the street.

Because of Tom's presence in front of the museum, I had to take a circuitous route back to my friends. I walked three blocks to the library, then looped around behind the building and walked through the parking lots until I got back to the museum.

When I returned to the front of the museum, I could barely see Sylvester. He had magically camouflaged himself next to the side of the front steps. Hob and Nob stood next to him as they awaited my return.

"What did he say?" Sylvester asked.

"He's been assigned to guard the museum all night," I reported.

When I glanced around Sylvester, I could see Tom standing next to the police cruiser. Tom was looking toward the park across the street.

"Even if the officer was not stationed here, I don't know how we would get past the electronic security system that guards the front entrance," Sylvester said. "Perhaps the loading dock is our best option. If an alarm sounds, we can retreat into the canal."

"It's probably a silent alarm," I said. "We wouldn't even know that we set it off."

"Nob and I can squeeze through very small spaces," Hob said. "We might be able to enter the building through the mailbox. If we can't get in that way, there should be an air vent or some other opening that we can use to get in."

"We can find magical items in the museum and then bring those outside so that all of us can closely examine them. When we are finished, we can return the items to their correct places in the museum -- except for the item sought by the sorcerer. I suppose that we'll need to remove that item so that he can't get it."

"That is a good plan," I said. "If an alarm is activated or a guard enters the room, you could simply assume your statue disguises."

"I like their plan, too," Sylvester said. "However, some items like the sword and helmet will likely be too large to remove through the narrow opening by which you gain entrance."

Suddenly, the elfstone attached to Sylvester's belt began to glow bright red and emit a humming sound. He looked startled as he pulled the stone off his belt and stared at it.

"What's happening?" I asked nervously.

"All the wardstones that I've placed along the border of this town are glowing!" he exclaimed. "The sorcerer has crossed the border and is heading this way! Caroline, you and the gnomes need to get away from here! Now!"

"I should warn Tom Coogan," I said. "He has no idea what is coming this way! He needs to get away, too"

As I glanced toward where Tom stood by his police cruiser, I realized that he had not moved since I had looked in his direction thirty seconds earlier. He was as motionless like a tall garden gnome.

"Look!" I pointed toward Tom. "He's frozen in a statue-like pose."

Sylvester's face became alarmed. "Black magic! The sorcerer is here! Run, Caroline! Run, Nob and Hob!"

Chapter 6 – Signal to Sagehorn

At that moment, a tall, dark figure emerged from the park across the street. With a complete confidence, he strode across the street. He did not even bother to glance at the immobilized police officer.

"There's no need to continue hiding over there, troll," he declared. "I can see you and your little friends quite clearly."

"Run to the canal," Sylvester whispered to me before walking forward to confront the sorcerer.

"I am not hiding from you, sorcerer! You have no business in this town! I command you to leave!"

The sorcerer laughed contemptuously. "Out of my way, fool!"

"We are children of the Light. We want no commerce with you, creature of the Dark."

"I care not what you want, troll!" The sorcerer continued his advance.

Sylvester held his ground, blocking the sorcerer's path into the museum. From beneath his billowing robes, the sorcerer pulled a staff. He raised the staff, and it emitted a power beam that struck Sylvester, knocking him twenty feet through the air. He landed hard on the museum's portico. The ground shook with the impact of his landing.

When the sorcerer's malevolent eyes turned in my direction, a chill ran through the length of my body. I realized that Hob and Nob were pulling on my legs, trying to get me to move.

"Come on, Caroline!" Hob implored me. "Sylvester told us to get you out of here!"

"We need to get into the canal, then back to your bike at the bridge!" Nob added as he continued to tug on my other leg.

I was conflicted about what to do. Sylvester wanted the gnomes and me to get away as quickly as possible. However, I did not want to leave him alone against the sorcerer.

"There is nothing that we can do to help him!" Hob said as if reading my mind.

"The sorcerer could take you as a hostage to use against Sylvester!" Nob said.

I turned and ran with the gnomes toward the parking lot behind the museum. They had convinced me that I would be doing a disservice to Sylvester by remaining. It seemed likely that I would be taken as a hostage. My only superpower was discernment of truth. In the middle of a battle, that power was not particularly useful.

We were about halfway across the parking lot when we spotted them. A half-dozen forms came scampering out of the canal.

I stopped and stared. "What is coming toward us?"

"Hobgoblins!" Nob exclaimed, a look of consternation appearing on his face.

"We can't go that way!" Hob shouted.

"Why are they here?" I asked as we ran back toward the front of the museum.

"They serve the sorcerer," Nob explained. "He brought them with him tonight."

We reached the front steps just in time to see Sylvester hurl a brick at the sorcerer. A brick thrown with such force would likely have killed an ordinary man, but the sorcerer's staff seemed to generate an energy field that protected him. The brick deflected harmlessly away.

The sorcerer slammed his staff against the portico and another power beam radiated into Sylvester. He was slammed into the outer wall with great force, sending vibrations through the entire museum.

Sylvester reminded me of the Incredible Hulk superhero from the movies. However, unlike the Hulk, Sylvester was completely in control of himself and his actions.

I felt small hands grabbing at my legs and arms. The hobgoblins had caught us.

"Let go of me!" I shouted.

Fortunately, I was much larger than all of the hobgoblins, who ranged in size from two to three feet tall. I kicked and threw several of the hobgoblins onto the lawn. They were unhurt, but they now looked at me warily and did not attempt to seize me again.

Hob and Nob were smaller than the hobgoblins. The two gnomes fought against the hobgoblins, but the gnomes were overwhelmed until I intervened on their behalf. I tossed three more of the hobgoblins onto the lawn with their companions.

"Now stay away from us or I'm going to beat you up!" I warned them.

They conferred amongst themselves, undoubtedly planning strategy. If they all swarmed me at once, they could overwhelm me, so we needed to be ready to run.

I decided that it would be wise to put some additional distance between us and the hobgoblins.

"Let's go up on the portico," I said to the gnomes.

While we ran up the ramp, I glanced over at Sylvester who was back on his feet and fighting the sorcerer. From some hidden pocket, Sylvester pulled a spiked ball and hurled it at the sorcerer, who raised his staff in order to deflect it with magic.

However, somehow the spiked ball was impervious to the black magic. Perhaps Sylvester's weapon had been anointed or created in such a way that magic had no effect upon it.

The spiked ball went through the force field as though it was not present. The weapon slammed into the sorcerer's left shoulder, its spikes cutting him badly. The sorcerer looked startled as he fell backward, clutching his wounded shoulder.

As Sylvester charged at him, the sorcerer's staff emitted a bright orange power beam. A glow wrapped itself around Sylvester like a net, and he was immobilized like the police officer, Tom Coogan.

However, perhaps because Sylvester was so much larger than Tom or perhaps because he understood the nature of the magic, Sylvester was able to resist the full effects of the spell. He could move neither his legs nor most of his upper body, but he retained some mobility in his hands. Sylvester pulled the wardstone off his belt and crushed it in his hands.

There was an explosion of blue light accompanied by a loud chime like the sound of a bell. The sparkling dust remnants of the stone floated to the ground.

"Well played," the sorcerer said, "By destroying an elfstone, you sent a signal to Sagehorn. However, the elves won't get here in time."

"One can always hope," Sylvester said dryly.

"Not those who incur my wrath. They can abandon all hope."

"You overestimate yourself, proud sorcerer."

"Statues aren't supposed to speak," the sorcerer said and again used his staff to wrap a magical glow around Sylvester.

This time the statue spell took full effect, causing Sylvester to become as still as Tom Coogan. The troll looked like a giant garden gnome.

Having successfully neutralized Sylvester, the sorcerer's attention turned toward gaining entry to the museum. He aimed his staff at the museum's heavy oak doors. The sorcerer fired a power beam that shattered the doors.

Splinters and wood fragments rained down upon the gnomes and me since we were standing just a few feet from the entrance. The remnants of the doors hung limply upon their hinges.

The sorcerer strode forward toward the entrance. Because he was coming almost directly toward us, the gnomes and I ran into the museum. All the lights were on. Probably they left the lights on overnight as a security precaution to help any officers on patrol in the museum.

The gnomes followed me as I led them though the main hall. We dashed behind the information counter.

A few seconds later the sorcerer walked into the main hall. His cold eyes briefly focused upon me. For a second, I feared that the sorcerer was about to turn his wrath upon the gnomes and me.

However, then he looked away from me as he scanned the room. The gnomes and I were apparently not of any interest to him. He had decided that we were unimportant, so he ignored us. The sorcerer walked to the center of the room, then glanced back at the hobgoblins, who were hovering near the shattered front doors.

"Come inside and find what I seek," he commanded them.

The hobgoblins swarmed into the museum. It was evident that they had been given a specific assignment. They quickly split into groups as they went through the three doorways connected to the main hall.

While his minions were away on their mission, the sorcerer casually inspected the large fountain in the center of the room. Multi-colored spotlights illuminated the fountain. In front of the cascading wall of water, there was a statue of a beautiful woman. Her right foot was slightly raised as she prepared to crush the head of a serpent.

During these few peaceful minutes, I again observed the large banner promoting the Aztec exhibit. The exhibit had arrived three weeks ago and was scheduled to remain in this museum for another three weeks before the exhibit moved to another city.

In an instant, I saw the truth of the situation. I should have made this realization during my previous visit, and I silently berated my thickheaded stupidity.

The truth was so obvious. The Aztec exhibit was why the sorcerer was here now. What he wanted was here now. It was not chance that had brought him to this museum at this time. He could not have come here two years ago or two years from now because the Aztec exhibit was the only thing of interest to him.

More specifically -- something in the exhibit was of great interest to him. I recalled what I had read on the educational story cards next to the Aztec artworks. The Aztecs had performed ritual killings in which men, women, and children were sacrificed to different pagan gods and goddesses. Of course, something from that culture of death would be what the sorcerer wanted.

The elfstone had reacted to four objects in the Aztec collection -- to the mask, the jade figurine, the obsidian knife, and the moonstone.

When the hobgoblins returned, they carried the mask, the jade figurine, the obsidian knife, and the moonstone. They handed the objects to the sorcerer.

"Good work," he praised them.

"We are glad that you are pleased, Molechson," the hobgoblin said, beaming with pride.

The sorcerer looked at him coldly. "I told you never to use my name when we are in the human world."

The hobgoblin looked fearful as he bowed and backed away. "I am sorry … sir. I became overexcited about what we found, and I forgot your orders."

"See that it never happens again. You are expendable and easily replaced."

"Yes, sir." The hobgoblin moved toward the back of his group, trying to get out of Molechson's sight.

The sorcerer turned and looked directly at me. "Seize the girl and the gnomes. We are going to bring them with us."

Darn! I had hoped that by staying out of his way, the sorcerer would continue to ignore us. I hoped that he would simply leave with the moonstone and other Aztec items. No such luck, though.

All the hobgoblins moved menacingly toward us. There were now at least twenty in their group, and I knew that we had no chance against so many of them. However, I would not be captured without a fight.

I noticed the group now included six larger hobgoblins who had not been among those against whom we fought outside a short while ago. These six larger hobgoblins wielded clubs.

This situation could not get any worse, I thought with a sigh.

Two seconds later, Helen came walking through the front entrance. I sighed more loudly. Of course things could get worse -- they can always get worse.

Helen slowly walked toward the center of the main hall. She wore a black evening gown that I recognized as my mother's gown. Helen had apparently gone into my parents' bedroom and taken the gown out of the closet.

While I was distracted by Helen's arrival, the hobgoblins rushed forward to seize me. The six larger hobgoblins grabbed me while their smaller companions grabbed the gnomes. They pushed us toward the sorcerer.

However, his attention was now focused entirely upon Helen. She stopped and stood before him.

"You summoned me, my love," Helen cooed. "My dreams have all been about you."

He stepped forward and placed his right hand upon her cheek. "I knew that you would come, my beauty. The meddlesome elves tried to keep us apart, but their plan failed. You are mine. And the gem that the elves tried to deny me is now mine, too."

He grasped the staff and carefully removed the small gem from its tip. After placing that gem into a pocket in his vest, he attached the moonstone to the staff. Because the moonstone was larger than the other stone, he had to adjust the mounting brackets. When he had finished, he looked at the staff with its new magical stone.

"Not a perfect fit, but it will do for now. Later tonight I will adjust the bracket so that the fit will be perfect."

"As will our lives, darling," Helen said.

"Helen, listen to me!" I shouted. "You are not in love with that man! You don't even know him! He is an evil sorcerer! He has placed a spell on you that has confused you!"

"Silence!" he bellowed.

Helen looked over at me. "You are an adorable child. You are the cutest child that I have ever seen."

"Do you recognize me? I am Caroline -- your sister!"

The sorcerer closed his fingers into a fist. I started choking. After about ten seconds, he opened his hand, and I was able to breathe.

"If you speak again, it will be the last time that you speak," he warned me.

Apparently the sorcerer did not need the staff in order to wield his magic. The staff seemed to focus and intensify his powers, but he could wield magic without it.

"My name is now Helena," my sister told me before turning back toward the sorcerer.

He took hold of her left hand and grasped it possessively. "Come, Helena. It is time for us to leave. I now have both you and the moonstone -- the two treasures for which I came to this town."

The sorcerer led Helen across the main hall toward the far side. I was puzzled about where they were going because they were walking toward a marble wall.

When Molechson raised his staff and began chanting, his intentions became clear. The marble wall started to glimmer and lose its solidity. A glowing, translucent mist replaced the solid wall. The sorcerer had created a gateway to some other place -- perhaps to some other world.

"No, Helen! Stop!" I shouted as I ran forward, heedless of the danger.

I was determined to stop her. If Helen walked with him through that magical gateway, I doubted whether I would ever see her again.

Helen paused and looked over at me, confusion evident upon her face.

"We must leave now, Helena," the sorcerer said tersely, tightly grasping her hand as he urged her forward.

At that moment, the large fountain in the center of the room underwent a dramatic change. The water flow suddenly increased abundantly overflowing the stone sides of its pool. A bluish emerald color shone brightly from the waters. Another gateway was opening.

It all happened so fast. A tall, strong man bearing a shield on his left forearm and a sword in his right hand came leaping through the curtain of water. He was immediately followed by an athletic-looking man wielding a sword in his left hand. Two seconds later, a beautiful woman with a bow and arrow came through the watery gateway.

Instantly I knew who they were -- the elves had arrived.

The sorcerer cursed loudly. Molechson had known that Sylvester had sent the elves a signal by crushing an elfstone, but the sorcerer had not expected the elves to arrive so soon. The sorcerer had expected to be long gone from this town before the elves got here.

Almost immediately the elves spotted the enemy. The elf maiden shot a silver arrow from her golden bow. The arrow would have gone through the sorcerer's heart, but his magic deflected it. The arrow did not miss him completely, though. It grazed the same shoulder that Sylvester had wounded earlier that evening.

Howling with rage, Molechson raised his staff and fired a power beam at the elf maiden just as she was firing a second arrow at him. The power beam vaporized the arrow, then struck the elf maiden, knocking her through the air. She landed hard against a bench, temporarily stunned and out of the fight.

The elf with the shield charged at the sorcerer. Before the elf could reach Molechson, the sorcerer's power beam slammed into the shield. I expected the shield to be vaporized like the arrow, but the shield somehow stayed intact. However, the elf was hurled backward and landed in the pool of the fountain.

The addition of the moonstone to the sorcerer's staff had increased the strength of the power beam. I was glad that Molechson had not had this moonstone during his fight against Sylvester. My troll friend was only temporarily immobilized, but Sylvester might have been killed if the sorcerer had possessed the moonstone earlier.

Holding his sword in front of him like a shield, the third elf raced forward. The sorcerer's power beam hit the sword, which absorbed the force of the beam. Within seconds, the blade of the sword became superheated and blazed with fire. The flames, though, did not consume the blade.

Nor did the flames deter the elf. In spite of the beam's power, this elf pressed forward toward his enemy. At that moment, I had an epiphany: this man was Sagehorn, the leader of the elves. I intuitively knew this to be the truth.

The sorcerer knew who he was, too. For the first time that evening, I detected a hint of fear in Molechson's face. I wondered whether he and Sagehorn had ever previously fought against each other.

As Sagehorn got closer and closer, the sorcerer looked for help. He glanced over at the hobgoblins.

"You are worthless creatures!" Molechson shouted. "Stop this elf! Attack now! All of you!"

The hobgoblins who had been holding me released me and rushed to join the other hobgoblins who were swarming onto Sagehorn. While continuing to block the power beam with the sword in his left hand, Sagehorn tried to swat away the hobgoblins with his right hand.

Sagehorn successfully defended himself until the larger hobgoblins crashed into him. Like defensive linemen in a football game tackling a quarterback, the larger hobgoblins knocked Sagehorn down.

A look of relief appeared on Molechson's face. Realizing that this was his window of opportunity, the sorcerer took firm hold of Helen's arm and propelled her forward toward the gateway that he had opened.

With horror, I watched my sister and the sorcerer walk through the glowing, translucent mist and disappear. All of the hobgoblins ran after their leader and jumped through the gateway.

Helen was gone. I struggled against the feelings of despair that threatened to overwhelm me.

The gateway began to close. The top of the wall changed from mist back into solid marble. Like a garage door coming down, the gateway began to shut from top to bottom. In a few seconds, the entire wall would be solid marble again.

A silver arrow slammed into the center of the wall directly below where the marble was still glowing mist. I glanced back across the main hall and saw the elf maiden holding the bow from which she had just fired the arrow.

"The arrow will only hold the gateway open for a few seconds!" she shouted as she ran forward.

As I ran toward the gateway, Hob and Nob followed me. Before I could go through it, though, Sagehorn grabbed me.

"Remain here, young lady!" he said. "It's too dangerous for you!"

"The sorcerer took my sister with him!" I implored him. "Please allow me to go with you."

"Sagehorn, we must go now!" the elf warrior with the shield exclaimed.

"Go, Rumlad!" Sagehorn ordered.

In response to his leader's command, Rumlad dashed through the gateway.

Just as he disappeared, the arrow holding the gateway open snapped. The wall's conversion back to marble resumed.

"No!" I screamed upon seeing that the opening was now less than three feet high.

Moving with incredible swiftness, Sagehorn scooped me up under his right arm. The elf maiden grabbed the two gnomes. With us as their passengers, Sagehorn and the woman hurled themselves toward the narrow opening.

They were horizontal as they went through the gateway. The speed and gracefulness of the elves was astonishing.

We came tumbling out of the gateway, landing in a mysterious place.

Chapter 7 – Through the Gateway

We emerged in the unlikeliest of places. At least I was very surprised. I had expected to emerge in a dark castle or creepy mansion. My suspicion was that the sorcerer and Dracula shared similar tastes. Wherever a vampire felt at home, the sorcerer would also feel comfortable and at home.

Instead, however, we emerged from the gateway onto a snowy mountain plateau. Sagehorn released me and stood up, brushing the snow off his clothing. Neither the sorcerer nor Helen were anywhere within sight.

The elf maiden stooped down in order to set Hob and Nob onto the ground. With wide eyes, the two gnomes looked around with great interest.

Sagehorn looked at me and the gnomes. "Young lady, what is your name? And who are these two gentlemen with you?"

"My name is Caroline Casey, sir. And my two friends are Hob and Nob."

"I'm pleased to meet you, Caroline, Hob, and Nob. My name is Sagehorn, and this is my sister, Sally. And the fine fellow with the shield is Rumlad."

"It's an honor to meet all of you," Nob said.

"Yes, we are very glad to meet you," Hob said in agreement.

"Caroline, Hob, and Nob -- I am pleased to meet you even under these strange circumstances in this unexpected place."

"Where are we?" I asked, looking around.

"In the mountains," Rumlad said.

"I can see that! I mean what mountains?"

"First we need to determine what world we are in," Rumlad said. "The sorcerer could have opened a gateway to a world of faerie or to other places."

"Do you mean that we might be in a faerie world?" I asked with astonishment.

"If this was a faerie world, there would likely be one or two dragons flying around those mountain peaks," Sally said. "I believe that we are still in the mortal world. I would suppose that we are in the Alps."

"Based upon the position of the sun, the time of day would seem to be consistent with the time difference between the Alps and the place from which we just departed," Rumlad said.

"And the temperature and flora suggest that this is the Alps," Sally added. "The Himalayan Mountains would be colder."

"It's plenty cold here," I said, shivering and rubbing my hands together to warm them.

"This might help a bit." Sagehorn took off his jacket and placed it on my shoulders.

"Thanks." I slipped my arms into the sleeves and immediately felt warmer. The jacket was made of some material that I could not identify.

"Won't you get cold without your jacket?" I asked him.

"No. We are not affected by heat and cold as much as humans. I have never been sick."

"What?"

"We don't get sick or grow old," Rumlad said.

"That's cool." I glanced down at Hob and Nob. "I suppose that you guys don't get sick or old either."

"That's right, Caroline," Nob said.

"And it's fortunate that we aren't bothered by heat and cold since we're outside almost all the time," Hob said, grinning broadly.

The three elves were looking up and down the mountain as they tried to decide which direction to go.

Rumlad pointed down toward the base of the mountain. "There is a village down in that valley far below us. Based upon what we know about the sorcerer's evil interests, he has likely been preying upon those villagers for his experiments and … other things."

"He might have taken Caroline's sister down to the village," Sally said. "If he is planning to force the young woman into being his bride, he could complete the charade by having a wedding in the village."

Sagehorn pointed toward the peak of the mountain on which we stood. "The shimmering up there near the summit suggests that something is magically concealed. It could be the sorcerer's lair. From this distance, it's difficult to say with certainty."

"I can see the shimmering!" I said. "It seems to surround some structure. I'll be that it is his lair!"

All three elves were clearly surprised by my observation.

"Caroline, I have never previously met a human who could see something magical," Sally said.

"Very impressive, Caroline," Sagehorn said. "Well, we need to decide whether to go down to the village or up to his lair. Up or down -- that is the question."

"To be or not to be -- that is a different question for a different day," Sally said with a grin as she recalled a Shakespeare quotation.

"The correct answer to the question posed by Shakespeare's Hamlet is 'to be' -- life is glorious and, when necessary, we 'take up arms against a sea of troubles, and by opposing, end them.' That is what we shall do today."

"The up-or-down question still needs to be resolved," Sally said.

"I believe that the sorcerer took the young lady up the mountain to his lair," Rumlad said.

"I agree," Sally said.

"As do we," Nob and Hob chimed in unison.

"As do I," Sagehorn said. "Upwards we go."

Because here was only a dusting of snow on the mountainside, Hob and Nob did not have any trouble walking up the slope. Concerned that they might grow tired, I offered to carry them, but they assured me that they were fine.

"We used to live in the Appalachian Mountains, Caroline," Nob told me.

"Yes, we like the mountains," Hob said.

"How did you and Nob become friends with Caroline?" Sally asked as we trudged up the slope.

"We have known Caroline since she was three years old," Hob explained. "While we were in the garden in our statue disguises, she began talking to us. Somehow she knew that we were alive."

"I can also see fairies," I added.

"Very few humans have the ability to see magical beings," Sally said. "You have been given a wondrous gift."

I nodded. "That's the way that I consider my ability."

"Caroline how did you and your sister become involved in this situation?" Sagehorn asked.

"When Helen and her friend did not return from the shopping mall yesterday evening, my father and I went searching for them and found them in the woods near the river. They were very confused and didn't know what happened to them. The gnomes had mentioned to me that a troll recently began spending most of his time at a bridge close to where we found the girls. I suspected that the troll might have been involved, so I went to see him."

"That was very brave, Caroline," Sagehorn said.

"Thank you. Anyway, after meeting Sylvester, I realized that he was a good man. He told me that you had sent him there in order to protect my town from an evil sorcerer. Sylvester and I figured out that what the sorcerer wanted was in our town's museum."

"How did you make that determination?" Sagehorn inquired.

"Three teenagers broke into the museum on the same night that Helen and her friend were spellbound. Sylvester thought that, because the sorcerer was reluctant to cross the wardstone boundary, he used black magic to force the teenagers to do his bidding. That's why we all went to museum. However, before we got inside, the sorcerer arrived and got into a big fight with Sylvester. You would have been proud of Sylvester."

"Sylvester fought well and bravely, but the sorcerer used his magic to freeze him into a statue pose." Hob interjected.

"We believe that the effects of the spell are temporary," Nob added. "He should be fine."

"The hobgoblins found the moonstone and some other things that the sorcerer wanted," I said. "Then my sister, Helen, came walking through the front entrance. I suppose that he used black magic to summon her there."

"We shall do our best to rescue your sister," Sagehorn promised.

"Thank you."

During the entire ascent, I felt like we were being watched. From somewhere within his lair, the sorcerer was using either magic or a telescope to watch our approach. And, while he watched, he was surely planning how to destroy us. Nevertheless, we would not be deterred from our mission.

As we continued the ascent, the slope became steeper. The gnomes and I struggled to keep pace with the elves. Soon I was breathing hard, and the gnomes were loudly huffing and puffing.

Upon reaching a plateau, Sagehorn paused and sat down on a rock ledge. He gestured for us to sit with him.

"Let's take a brief rest here," Sagehorn said.

I admired Sagehorn's kindness and discretion. I knew that the rest break was for the benefit of the gnomes and me. The three elves did not seem a bit tired. This ascent was clearly very easy for them.

"We're slowing you down," I said as I sat next to Sagehorn on the ledge. The gnomes hopped up beside me.

"Sagehorn, if you and Sally and Rumlad want to go faster, we can catch up with you on the mountaintop," Hob said. "Nob and I will keep Caroline safe."

"Hob and Nob, I know that you would keep Caroline safe. However, we are moving swiftly enough. We need to consider our path as we proceed. It is not wise to rush headlong into the mouth of the beast."

Sagehorn detached a thermos from his belt and handed the thermos to me. I enjoyed a refreshing drink of water. Until that moment, I did not realize how thirsty I was. While I drank, Sally and Rumlad gave some water to the gnomes.

I gave the thermos back to the elf prince. "Sagehorn, I was just remembering something that Sylvester told me. He said that someone who lives in a sorcerer's lair sent you a secret message that the sorcerer would be coming to my town."

Sagehorn nodded. "Yes. Apparently, we have an ally in the enemy's camp. Someone became so disgusted by the sorcerer's crimes that this person decided to change sides."

"That's good."

"Elves are the defenders of nature and the natural law," Sagehorn said. "Our secret ally knew that we would be willing to help."

As I glanced toward the mountain peak, I recalled what Sally had said about dragons in the faerie worlds.

"It would be wonderful to see a dragon," I said.

Sagehorn smiled. "There are some dragons that you would not want to get anywhere near. I have ridden a dragon into battle, and the magnificent creature won the day for us. However, on a darker day in a different world, another dragon's fiery breath almost turned me to ash."

"What other magical creatures actually exist?" I asked. "Are there leprechauns and unicorns and mermaids?"

He nodded. "Yes. Our Creator's imagination has no limit. Countless fantastic creatures and other beings have been brought into existence. Many of these beings are in the spiritual realm, but many others are in mortal worlds. There are worlds within worlds, dimensions within dimensions. Creation is wider and more glorious than any of us can conceive."

"Wow!"

"Do not underestimate the generosity of the Creator," Sagehorn said. "Indeed, his generosity cannot be overestimated. When you think that you have seen it all, remember that you've only seen a small fraction of creation. Over the next hill, there is always something new."

Chapter 8 – The Sorcerer's Lair

We resumed our trek up to the summit. A magical dome camouflaged the mountaintop lair beneath an illusion of heavy fog and snow.

A perceptive observer from the valley below might have questioned the perennial presence of the fog and snow. How could it snow unceasingly day after day? If anyone had ventured up to the mountaintop to investigate this strange phenomenon, it is likely that the person never returned to the valley.

We were getting close to the mountaintop. I squinted as I peered through the magical screen that concealed the sorcerer's lair. The bunker-like fortress was constructed of white stones that harmonized perfectly with the magical camouflage.

From the lower section of the fortress, I could see numerous figures emerging. Whether they were human or not, I could not tell from this distance. I was sure, though, that they were coming to intercept us.

The elves saw them, too. After briefly conferring with Sally and Rumlad, Sagehorn turned to me and the gnomes.

"The sorcerer is sending humans and hobgoblins to attack us. I don't want to kill them, so we are going to go around them. We can move too fast for them to stop us. However, it will be necessary for us to carry the three of you."

The gnomes and I readily agreed. I hopped onto Sagehorn's back and wrapped my arms around his neck for a piggyback ride to the mountaintop. Sally picked up Nob, while Rumlad scooped up Hob.

In a flash, we were gone. The speed at which the elves could run was truly amazing. We wove a path through the sorcerer's forces, moving with such speed that they could barely see us.

"What's that?" someone asked.

"What's what?" someone else replied.

I did not hear the rest of the conversation. In less than a minute, we reached the fortress wall. The elves headed directly toward the door through which the hobgoblins and humans had emerged.

By sending his minions after us, the sorcerer had inadvertently showed us a discrete way to enter his lair. We might never have noticed the small, secret door at the base of the structure. Now we had an easy way inside. It would not be necessary to go charging through the main entrance, which was surely well-protected, perhaps even with magical traps.

Going through the door, we went into the hallway. Rumlad locked the door behind us so that the sorcerer's minions could not get back inside that way.

"If we need to retreat, we can still get out this way," Rumlad said.

"Hopefully some of those humans and hobgoblins outside will take advantage of this opportunity to escape down into the valley below," Sally said.

"Let's hope so," Sagehorn agreed.

We cautiously walked further into the hallway. We were well aware that there could even be magical traps down here.

The place gave me the creeps. There was a feeling of wrongness here.

Rumlad, who was walking in the point position, looked back at Sagehorn.

"Do you want me to scout ahead?" Rumlad asked.

"Yes," Sagehorn replied.

Rumlad dashed down the hallway, vanishing around a corner. At a more moderate pace, we followed the same path.

"Do you think that the sorcerer has a fountain somewhere in this place?" Sally asked her brother.

"I doubt it." Sagehorn glanced at the storage rooms and utility rooms that lined the hallway. "This place is designed for practicality for achieving his evil purposes. Fountains and other things of beauty hold little interest to a person such as Molechson."

Sally nodded in agreement. "He only wanted the moonstone for the power imbued within it. The beauty of the stone itself is superfluous to such a person." She frowned. "There will be no fountain here."

As I listened to the discussion between Sally and her brother, I wondered why they cared whether or not there was a fountain here. At first I was puzzled, but then I experienced an epiphany. I saw the truth.

"Do you need a fountain in order to get us home?" I blurted out. "You arrived at the museum through a mystical gateway in the fountain?"

"I need at least a moderate amount of flowing water in order to create a gateway," Sagehorn said. "That fountain in the museum was barely large enough for me to open a gateway in it."

"In this world and in the faerie worlds, there are some large, permanent gateways in some oceans and lakes," Sally added. "We usually sail our ships through those gateways in order to travel from place to place. However, in order to get to your town, we needed to improvise a bit."

"That was the smallest gateway through which we have ever traveled," Sagehorn said. "When Sylvester sent us a signal by smashing the wardstone, we knew that something was very wrong and that we needed to get there as soon as possible. I opened a gateway as close as I could to the source of the signal."

"Caroline, you have been too polite to ask, but I'm sure that you have been wondering why only three elves responded to the distress signal," Sally said.

"It did cross my mind," I admitted.

"We planned to bring many warriors with us, but the gateway was so small that we could only pass through one at a time," she said. "We did not expect to come under immediate attack. When the sorcerer fired a power beam at me, the beam caused the gateway to collapse."

"So just the three of us got through the gateway," Sagehorn said. "Hopefully we will suffice for accomplishing what needs to be done."

"I sure that you will," I said.

Just as we reached a stairwell, Rumlad came running up the stairs. He stood in front of Sagehorn as he gave his report.

"On the level beneath us, there are some dungeons in which about twenty persons are imprisoned. Next to the dungeons, there is a laboratory in which the sorcerer's assistants and apprentices conduct gruesome experiments. What do you want me to do?"

"We need to free those prisoners," Sagehorn said. "I would assume that most of them are from the village at the base of this mountain. As soon as the prisoners are safely away from here, we will destroy the laboratory so that no more atrocities can occur there. Sally can help you with this task. In the meantime, Caroline, the gnomes, and I will go upstairs and find Helen."

"I can handle the situation downstairs by myself," Rumlad said. "You will likely need Sally's help upstairs against the sorcerer."

"Very well," Sagehorn said. "Join us upstairs when you are finished."

While Rumlad went back to the dungeon, the rest of us headed up the stairwell. I wondered whether there was some sort of video surveillance system. It was more likely, I suppose, that the sorcerer was using a crystal ball or some other magical means to watch us.

We emerged from the stairwell and entered a large, cavernous room illuminated by torches along the walls. In the shadows, I could see something moving.

"I knew that I was going to be in the creepy castle sooner or later," I said in a whisper to the gnomes.

"The sooner that we're out of here, the better," Hob said, looking around nervously.

Near the center of the room, there was a large sculpture of a feathered serpent.

I heard a loud click that sounded like a door opening. Seconds later, the sorcerer and Helen walked into the far side of the room. He held Helen's arm like she was a possession rather than a person.

The sorcerer looked at us contemptuously. "Look, Helena. A ragtag group of trespassers has entered our home."

"Helen, this is not your home!" I shouted. "The sorcerer is using black magic to control your mind."

Helen looked at me. "My name is Helena," she said tersely.

"Your name is Helen Casey," I insisted. "Do you remember when Father and I found you and Amy wandering in the woods by the river? The sorcerer placed a spell on you and Amy. Helen, you know that I have a special ability to discern truth and lies. When have I ever been wrong?"

"Never," she admitted.

"That is correct. And I have discerned the truth here: he is using black magic to control your mind."

"Shut up!" the sorcerer shouted.

While I spoke with Helen, I noticed Sally inconspicuously take an arrow out of the quiver and notch the arrow in her bow. Now she fired the arrow directly at the sorcerer's heart.

This arrow, however, bounced off the magical force field that guarded him. He raised his staff, and a beam of white light radiated from the moonstone. When the beam struck Sally, she had already notched another arrow and had drawn back the bow in preparation for firing. However, the beam froze her into a statue pose.

I was momentarily reminded of a statue of Diana. Like Diana from Roman mythology, Sally looked like a graceful, beautiful, and athletic warrior -- a warrior completely removed from the present battle.

With his sword drawn, Sagehorn charged toward the sorcerer. As he ran across the room, I suddenly noticed the magical trap in the center of the room.

"Sagehorn! Stop!" I shouted.

It was too late. An 8-foot-wide hole in the floor was magically camouflaged. Sagehorn tried to stop, but he had already stepped over the edge. He fell into the hole.

Horrified, I ran forward to the edge of the hole and looked down. Sagehorn lay at the bottom of a pit in which there was a monster.

The creature was huge. It was about sixteen feet tall, and it had three heads. At first I assumed that it was a hydra that the sorcerer had brought here from some faerie dimension in some magical world.

As I looked more closely at the creature's face, I saw its true nature. It was a Komodo dragon. The sorcerer had somehow altered the nature of the reptile, causing it to become many times larger, grow two additional heads, and become more aggressive.

"My hydra has not been fed yet today," the sorcerer said in malicious glee. "Your elf friend will be a delicious meal for him."

When Sagehorn tried to stand up, the creature raised all three of its heads in preparation for attack.

I didn't see what happened next because, at that moment, some unseen power locked onto me and lifted me high into the air. The sorcerer was holding me with a power beam. For a few seconds, I was afraid that he intended to drop me into the pit so that I would be killed there, too.

However, using the power beam, he carried me away from the pit and placed me upon a stone table that was about ten feet from where he stood with Helen.

"The Aztecs realized that much power could be gained as a result of carrying out human sacrifices," Molechson declared. "You will be our sacrifice today."

He pulled a knife from a pocket in his vest. I recognized the knife as one of the Aztec art objects that he had stolen from the museum.

The sorcerer handed the knife to my sister. "Helena, you will have the honor of conducting the ritual."

I watched Helen slowly walk toward me with the intention of killing me. I could no longer see the power beam with which the sorcerer placed me on the table, so I tried to get up and run away. However, some unseen power pressed me down upon the table.

My beloved sister reached the table and looked down upon me. I was filled with profound sadness. My parents were going to lose two daughters today: I was about to die upon this pagan altar, and Helen would apparently be spending the rest of her life with the sorcerer.

My parents would not know what happened to us. Tom Coogan, the police officer who was Helen's soccer coach, would be able to tell my parents that he saw me in town buying a snow cone on Main Street. I don't know whether anyone saw Helen as she walked from our home to the museum.

My parents would probably think that we had been abducted by some psycho. In a way, I suppose that we were.

My poor parents -- I mourned for my parents.

And I mourned for Helen. She was about to kill me. If Helen ever comes out of this stupor and realizes what she has done, she will be filled with unbearable grief. Even though Helen is not always nice to me, I know that she loves me. Knowing that she killed me will be terrible for her. Somehow she will have to find a way to go forward with her life.

With her left hand, Helen pushed my head against the table. With her right hand, she raised the knife above her head as she prepared to carry out the sacrifice to a demon.

"Helen, wait!" I implored her. "I want to tell you something important -- I love you! I don't know whether you will be able to remember anything that I say, but try to imprint this upon your memory. I forgive you for what you are about to do. I know that you are not doing this out of your own free will. This evil man controls you now, but his control is temporary. Someday we will be reunited, and we will be together forever. Our love is forever. Love is stronger than any sorcerer's spell. You are Helen Casey, my sister -- and I love you. No matter what happens here today, always remember that truth."

"Kill her now!" the sorcerer bellowed.

Helen turned and looked at him. "No," she said quietly and threw the knife across the room.

The sorcerer became enraged. "How dare you defy me? You shall join your sister on the altar of sacrifice!"

He glanced down at the numerous hobgoblins who had gathered near him.

"Bring me that knife!" he ordered.

Suddenly there was a loud explosion from the level below, causing the entire building to shake.

"Find out what is going on down there!" the sorcerer commanded a hobgoblin, who went running to investigate.

Meanwhile, another hobgoblin retrieved the Aztec knife and ran back to Molechson. However, as the sorcerer reached out to take the knife, the hobgoblin stabbed him in the back of the knee.

The hobgoblin drove the knife deep into the knee. He then pulled it out and dashed across the room.

The sorcerer howled with pain. He dropped his staff and grabbed his wounded leg.

Without hesitation, I jumped off the table and ran toward him. I grabbed the staff and ran to the opposite side of the room. I stood next to Hob and Nob and the hobgoblin who had stabbed Molechson.

The sorcerer chanted some words and a glow appeared around his hands, which he pressed against his knee. I realized that he was trying to use magic to heal the wound.

I held the staff high and willed for it to fire a power beam at Molechson. However, nothing happened.

The sorcerer looked over at me and laughed mockingly. "Possessing the staff doesn't do you any good if you don't know how to use it."

Limping on his wounded leg, he staggered toward me.

"It is I with whom you must deal, sorcerer!" Sagehorn called out as he pulled himself out of the pit into which he had been thrown.

Upon seeing him, I was filled with joy. Sagehorn stood there holding his gleaming sword. I looked upon him with profound admiration. He was an almost perfect man. He was like Adam before the Fall.

Molechson stared at Sagehorn with disbelief. "How can you be alive?"

"The creature gave me a good fight, but I cut off all three of it heads."

There were two thunderous explosions beneath us, and the room shook violently. Large sections of the walls and ceiling collapsed around us.

A slab of concrete fell upon the statue of the feathered serpent, smashing the statue into bits. It reminded me of someone stepping on a snake in the garden.

"What have you done, elf?" the sorcerer hissed.

"Apparently my friend, Rumlad, has set your laboratories ablaze," Sagehorn said.

"Meddlesome elf, my revenge shall be terrible."

"Sorcerer, you are not sovereign, and your will is not supreme. You are a creature, not the Creator."

At that moment, Rumlad came running into the room. Sagehorn glanced over at him.

"Were you able to free all the prisoners?" Sagehorn asked.

"Yes. I led them out of the building and showed them a good path to take down the mountain to the village in the valley. Most of the hobgoblins have also fled from this building."

"Good work, Rumlad," Sagehorn praised him.

While they were speaking, the sorcerer's knee apparently had continued to heal. With surprising speed, Molechson ran at me, lunging toward the staff as he attempted to grab it.

I tossed the staff to Sagehorn. When the elf prince caught the staff, I saw fear in the face of the sorcerer.

"In case you are wondering," Sagehorn said with a slight grin, "I do know how to use it."

A green beam of light projected from the staff toward Sally. Instantly, she was freed from the statue spell. As mobility returned to her limbs, she spotted the sorcerer. Sally turned toward him with the intention of firing the arrow in her bow.

However, at that second, a huge explosion tore open most of the floor, knocking all of us off our feet. The sorcerer fell into the fiery chasm opened by the explosion.

As he seemed to be falling toward his death, I saw him reach into the pocket of his vest and pull out a gem. It was the gem that had been in his staff before he replaced it with the more powerful moonstone.

There was a flash of light, and I lost sight of him in the intense flames. I could not tell whether he teleported away or was consumed by the fire. In either case, he was gone.

Chapter 9 – The Journey Home

"Sagehorn, I estimate that this entire building will collapse in twenty to thirty seconds," Rumlad said with astonishing calmness. "I see that you have gained possession of the sorcerer's staff. If you can use it to open a gateway, now would be a good time."

"Don't you need flowing water?" I asked anxiously.

"If I did not have this staff, I would need flowing water," Sagehorn said. "However, since he used this staff to open a gateway here, I can reverse his gateway in order to get you home."

"Ten seconds until structure collapse, my prince," Rumlad reminded him.

"Be at peace, good Rumlad," Sagehorn said with a smile. "All is well."

Sagehorn aimed the staff at a section of the wall that was still intact. Instantly a swirling, emerald mist replaced the wall.

Sagehorn gestured for Helen and me to go through first. We were followed by the gnomes and the hobgoblin who had helped us. Rumlad, Sally, and Sagehorn jumped through the gateway a few seconds before the building imploded.

I sighed with relief upon finding myself back in the museum in my town. Without hesitation, Sagehorn pulled the moonstone out of the staff, then broke the staff in half. He tossed the two halves into the gateway where they were destroyed in the fires of the maelstrom. The force of the explosion caused the gateway to slam shut.

Sagehorn looked at my sister. "How are feeling, Helen?"

"I'm starting to feel better," she replied. "Thank you."

"It will take a while for the effects of the spell to wear off completely," Sagehorn told her. "I'm sure that Caroline will do a good job taking care of you. You are fortunate to have such a wonderful sister."

"Caroline is wonderful," Helen agreed as I tried not to blush.

Sagehorn bent down to shake hands with the hobgoblin. "Am I correct in assuming that you are the fine fellow who sent me the message alerting me about the sorcerer's scheme?"

"I am, sir," the hobgoblin said.

"And he stabbed the sorcerer in the back of his knee," I chimed in. "Stabbing him caused the sorcerer to drop his staff so that I was able to grab it."

"Good work," Sagehorn said. "What is your name?"

"My name is Winkin, sir."

"I will see that you are rewarded for your service, Winkin. You may go with us to Elvenhome."

"I have always wanted to go there!" Winkin beamed with joy.

"My friends!" Sylvester's voice boomed from across the room as he entered the museum. "I'm so glad that you are safe!"

All of us hurried over to greet him. We gave him a quick summary of everything that had happened.

"Destroying the staff must have released me from the statue spell," Sylvester said. "About three minutes ago, I was able to move normally again."

"I know the policeman who was also frozen by a statue spell," I said. "Is he all right?"

"Yes, as I was entering this museum, I looked back and saw that he was starting to move again," Sylvester said. "Fortunately, I got inside before he noticed me."

"Many persons will soon be coming into this museum, so we must leave in a few minutes," Sagehorn said. He held up the moonstone. "I am going to perform a blessing that will exorcise the evil power from this moonstone. Then I shall return it to the exhibit from which the sorcerer stole it."

When the moonstone was back in its previous place in the exhibit, we all prepared to leave the museum. Sylvester planned to remain in town for a few days. We made plans for a reunion in a few months. The elves were going to bring us to visit Elvenhome!

After saying goodbye to us, Sagehorn created a gateway in the flowing waters of the museum's fountain. Helen, Sylvester, Hob, Nob, and I waved goodbye to the elves and Winkin just before they passed through the mystical gateway.

Sylvester walked us home, then returned to his room beneath the town's library.

Everything was returning to normal -- at least as normal as it ever got in my world. The gnomes were in their usual spots in the garden. Helen was upstairs getting ready for her soccer game. Her coach, Tom Coogan, would be at that game at the soccer park. My mother, father, and I would be in the bleachers watching.

It had been an exciting adventure, but I hope that next weekend will be a bit less eventful -- and that's the truth.

****

Joseph Rogers has written the following stories, novels, and plays.

Novels:

Realm of Haden: A Space-Age Fantasy

Maiden of Orleans: A Bayou Thriller

The Snow Maiden: A Suspense Thriller

Moonlight Warriors: A Tale of Two Hit Men

The Powers That Be: A Supernatural Thriller

Stories:

Hallowed Eve, Hallowed Day: a supernatural suspense story

A Princess and her Five Suitors: a fairy tale

Sprite of the Light: a fairy tale

Plays:

Child of Wonder: a modern Christmas drama

Tobias, a Traveler: a drama in two acts

Garden Sanctuary

My Friend's Obsession

The Sword of St. Louis: a romantic drama in three short acts

Who Said It?: a whodunnit in two acts

The author's website is **JoeRogers.homestead.com**

Made in the USA
San Bernardino, CA
03 September 2015